Dear Parents:

Children learn to read in stages, and all children develop reading skills at different ages. **Ready Readers**™ were created to promote children's interest in reading and to increase their reading skills. **Ready Readers**™ are written on two levels to accommodate children ranging in age from three through eight. These stages are meant to be used only as a guide.

Stage 1: Preschool-Grade 1
Stage 1 books are written in very short, simple sentences with large type. They are perfect for children who are getting ready to read or are just becoming familiar with reading on their own.

Stage 2: Grades 1-3
Stage 2 books have longer sentences and are a bit more complex. They are suitable for children who are able to read but still may need help.

All the **Ready Readers**™ tell varied, easy-to-follow stories and are colorfully illustrated. Reading will be fun, and soon your child will not only be ready, but eager to read.

Mom's Day Off

Written by Eugene Bradley Coco

Illustrated by Colette Van Mierlo

Modern Publishing
A Division of Unisystems, Inc.
New York, New York 10022

Our mom works hard.

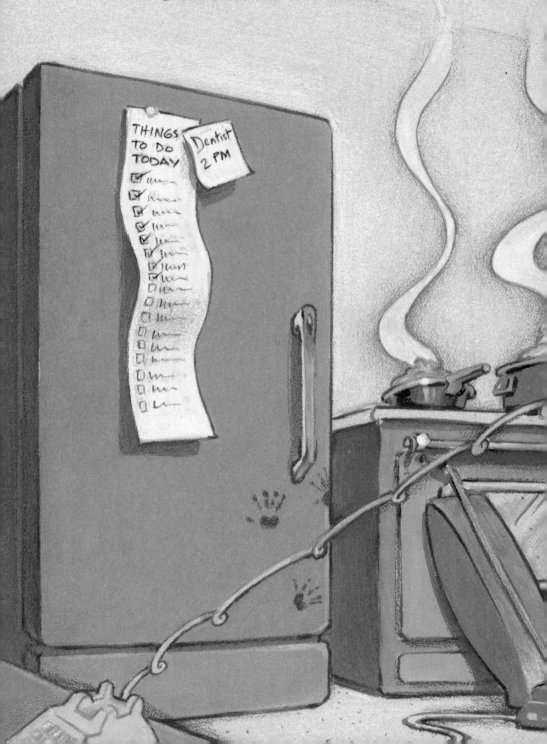

She cooks.

She cleans.

She sews our clothes
when they rip.

She takes care of us
when we're sick.

She even helps with
our homework.

Today Mom looks tired.

"Take the day off,"
we tell her.

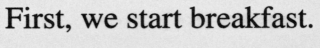

First, we start breakfast.
"Oh, no! Watch the eggs!"
I shout.

Mom helps us clean up.

Next we straighten up the den.

Sally starts to sweep.

There is so much dust.

Mom helps us clear the dust.

Soon it's time for Ginger's bath.
I turn on the water.

Sally gets Ginger.

The tub is almost full.

"Wait! The faucet is stuck!"

I scream.

Here comes Mom.

The laundry is next.

We put the clothes in the
machine and add soap.
Sally turns on the washer.

Oops!

The door isn't closed.

"Mom!" we yell.
Mom helps us pick up
the clothes.

Being in charge is hard work.
"Why don't you take the
rest of the day off?"
says Mom.

Thanks, Mom.